Parallel

An In-House Publication

Ukiyoto Publishing

All global publishing rights are held by

Ukiyoto Publishing
Published in 2023

Content Copyright © Ukiyoto
ISBN 9789360161590

All rights reserved.
No part of this publication may be reproduced, transmitted, or stored in a retrieval system, in any form by any means, electronic, mechanical, photocopying, recording or otherwise, without the prior permission of the publisher.

The moral rights of the author have been asserted.

This is a work of fiction. Names, characters, businesses, places, events, locales, and incidents are either the products of the author's imagination or used in a fictitious manner. Any resemblance to actual persons, living or dead, or actual events is purely coincidental.

This book is sold subject to the condition that it shall not by way of trade or otherwise, be lent, resold, hired out or otherwise circulated, without the publisher's prior consent, in any form of binding or cover other than that in which it is published.

www.ukiyoto.com

Contents

The Resonance	1
Painful Hearts	4
Conflicts in Fear	7
The Vendetta	9
Dangerous Subconscious	13
The Revise	19
The Subconscious Realm	20
The Melodrama	38
The Restoration	43
Together	44
The Insult	50
The Parallel	59

The Resonance

"Some places often reverberate the good and bad memories in your ears."

At the Railway Station

"Can I have some water? My throat hurts," she said, her voice hoarse.

This time the pain had subsided.

None of us chose to be born in this state.

Who are they to take away what is rightfully ours? This is our home, and we must fight for it.

Did Dipu get a job? Did he get it through his father's connections?

Cover your face, dude! We are going to fight for justice.

***

"Pankaj! Pankaj!" they called out.

"What are you looking at?" Srinu asked curiously.

"Just thinking about the past, as the train passes by," Pankaj replied with a smirk.

"The past?" Srinu exclaimed.

"Yeah, you see that *pan* shop over there?" Pankaj gestured with his eyes.

"What about it?" Srinu asked.

"Well, Pandit Saab is more famous than Assam tea," Pankaj said, and Srinu laughed along with him.

"Unknowingly, this Pandit Saab and this place, they created a mess in my life. These sounds and fragrances are dangerous. They bring back sleeping memories and make you realize, 'This is you!'" Pankaj grimaced.

"Did they remind you of something good or bad?" Srinu asked curiously, looking at Pankaj's face.

"Life! You see, life is a mysterious thing that no being is great enough to explain its essence. There was a time, right here at your age, where we chilled out to the core and cried to the end. But now, we forget the part of life unknowingly having the things that we fought for!" Pankaj blushed.

"You fought for life?" Srinu raised an eyebrow.

"Yeah, everyone must fight in life to grab their flying dreams," Pankaj replied nonchalantly.

"Your father works in the Railway department. He has a way to feed you all and fulfill your dreams. In the end, you have everything; unlike me and my father, who always barks at my face saying I'm useless when he does nothing to help me achieve my dreams," Srinu expressed his assumptions.

"Fathers are like that, Srinu. You know, you said your father barks at you. There was a time in my life where everything was good. I was chilling out with my friends, going to college, and traveling all over the state. But after completing my Masters, I understood what life is all about! It's not about what we studied or who we have behind us, but it's all about time. After completing my Masters, we started searching for employment. We searched for days, months, and years." Pankaj reminisced while having a conversation with Srinu.

Painful Hearts

"Unemployment is not just a word; it is a weighing stone that drags your soul down to the dark pitch."

"I knocked on thousands of doors for a single job, but I found that no door would open for me in my own land. Not just for me, but not even for my friends," Pankaj declared with drooping eyelids.

At Pandit's Shop

"I'm tired of looking for this!" Pankaj sighed with a sullen face.

"Didn't I tell you?" Dipu asked Pankaj, and then said, "Pandit Saab, two cigarettes."

"I can't understand a single thing, Dipu. I know I wrote well. I got around 80% when I calculated for the exam we recently took. I thought I was going to get it at any cost, but in the end, it just became a weight on my heart," Pankaj expressed his grief.

"You think just because you have knowledge you will get a job? Come on, man. Let's face reality. We live in a world where money, caste, religion, and especially bribes are all you need to get a job. We're lucky to be born without these things." Dipu smirked.

"Then why study so hard and spend lakhs on education? I feel like I'm useless," Pankaj exclaimed loudly.

"No man is useless. The system that man created is useless. But bro, without a doubt, I will be reborn as a dog. Pandit Saab will throw biscuits, and I can eat them for free." Rishi laughed and gave Dipu a high-five, staring at Pandit Saab's shop.

"Do one thing. Just watch my *pan* shop at night, and I will cancel all your debt from my shop," Pandit sarcastically taunted both Pankaj and Rishi.

"Okay, guys. I'll meet you tomorrow after the exam. I have to go home, or my father will be angry," Pankaj stated with a smile on his face and left the place in a hurry.

"Rishi, are you attending tomorrow's exam?" Dipu asked.

"I'm thinking about it. Anyway, we're not going to get it. There are only fifty places, which might already be taken. I've lost all hope. I'm preparing for the Ph.D. entrance. I'm not interested in this. Are you going?" Rishi said, chewing at his lower lip in worry.

"Do you think I will get the job? I won't waste my time on it. I have my own ways to secure a job," Dipu said as he puffed on his cigarette.

"Any plans for tomorrow?" Rishi asked eagerly.

"We'll meet here, along with Pankaj," Dipu replied with a smile directed at Rishi.

"Sure, I'll kidnap him and take him from the exam center. See you later," Rishi assured Dipu before walking away.

"Bye!" Dipu waved his hand before ordering a chilled beer from Pandit.

As Dipu drank and shouted at passing trains and commuters, Pankaj's father Goswami glared at his drunken state with anger. He decided to drop him off at his house. Dipu continued to rant on the way, shouting that fathers don't care about their sons' lives and only care about themselves. Goswami became frustrated and drove leisurely to Dipu's home. When Dipu's brother arrived, Dipu pushed him aside and went straight to his room. Vishwam thanked Goswami and left.

Conflicts in Fear

"When darkness seeps into a man's heart, he either rises to the sky or falls to the depths of the ocean."

At Home

After reaching home, Goswami washed his hands and feet, contemplating on how to convince his son to distance himself from Dipu and his group.

"Stop it, both of you!" Lakshmi intervened, trying to calm down the situation. "Pankaj, your father is just worried about your future. Goswami, you shouldn't accuse Pankaj without any proof!"

"Proof? What proof do I need? He's always with that Dipu and Rishi. Who knows what they do behind my back!" Goswami retorted.

"Dipu and Rishi are my friends, Papa. They are good people. Just because they don't have good jobs doesn't mean they are bad," Pankaj defended his friends.

"Fine, but you need to start thinking about your own future, Pankaj. You can't rely on your friends forever," Goswami said, trying to reason with his son.

"I know, Papa. I am trying. But it's not easy!" Pankaj sighed.

"Let's just have dinner and talk about this later. We are all tired and hungry," Lakshmi suggested, trying to diffuse the tension.

"What are you saying? I know you are not useless; you just can't understand your father's concern for you." Goswami grumbled at Pankaj.

"Not useless? Concern?" Pankaj shook his head in disbelief and pushed his food away before leaving the dining hall. He locked his door, crying heavily as he felt his insecurities getting triggered by his father's words. That night Pankaj went to bed with trembling hands and tears streaming down his face. His anxiety had reached a breaking point. He had lost control of his emotions.

The Vendetta

"Mysteriously! One person, one thought can change the world."

At the Examination Centre

"I hope no one has to go through that night again, because it marked the start of my downfall and adventures. But I woke up the next morning and prepared for the exam," Pankaj expressed to Srinu with a sense of disappointment.

"Yeah, tell me Dipu?" Rishi answered the call.

"Did you know this? Anyone from India can apply for this exam, and these people from Bihar are also here for the same exam!" Dipu exclaimed in anger.

"What? How is that possible? This is a state-level exam, only residents are eligible to apply!" Rishi was surprised to hear this.

"I don't know, but it's happening. This is unfair to us, the locals, who have been waiting for employment for so long. The government should do something about this!" Dipu expressed his frustration.

"Let's discuss this with our friends and take some action. We can't let this happen!" Rishi replied with determination.

"Yeah, let's do it. This is our fight for justice!" Dipu agreed and hung up the call.

"Stop it, Dipu! This is not the solution, and you know it!" Rishi interjected in a stern voice.

"Then what is the solution? Should we keep suffering while these vampires suck our blood?" Dipu retorted, his anger flaring up.

"We need to fight, but not like this. We need to raise our voice, organize ourselves, and demand our rights. Violence is never the answer," Rishi replied calmly.

"But who will listen to us? We are just a bunch of unemployed youth," Dipu argued.

"We will make them listen. We will unite and fight for our cause. But first, we need to believe in ourselves and in our strength," Rishi replied with determination.

Pankaj listened to their conversation silently, his mind still clouded by the pain and anger caused by his father's words. But as he listened to Rishi's words, a small glimmer of hope ignited in his heart. Maybe there was a way out of this darkness, a way to fight back against the injustice they faced every day.

"Okay, let's do it your way. Let's fight for our rights," Pankaj said, his voice filled with newfound determination.

Dipu and Rishi smiled, relieved that their friend had found a way out of his despair. Together, they formed a plan to organize a peaceful protest and demand their rights from the government. The road ahead would be long and arduous, but they were determined to see it through, no matter what challenges lay ahead.

"Shut up!" Dipu shouted at Rishi, encouraging Pankaj to take a sip of the alcohol. "Have a sip."

"Aaaah! It's hurting my throat! Water! Water!" Pankaj cried out, holding his throat and searching for water.

"You've lost your mind, Pankaj!" Rishi scolded him for trying to learn bad habits.

"We're here to fight against these vampires, not to have a wine party," Dipu claimed.

Dipu and his group had planned to destroy all the files of the Bihar students, attacking them with hockey bats and protesting them for taking their jobs. When they did exactly that, the situation turned fierce and chaotic, and the police intervened with *lathi* charges and smoke bombs to disperse the protestors. They ran fiercely and escaped from the cops.

As the birds hummed and the sun rose, the streets of Assam echoed with the voices of people demanding their rights, and fighting for their future. They held red flags and placards, and protested through marches and demonstrations.

"Were you a part of the protest too?" Srinu asked Pankaj, surprised.

"Yes, we fought fiercely for our future!" Pankaj said proudly.

"What happened after the fight?" Srinu asked Pankaj with renewed interest.

"From then on, we struggled a lot for jobs. My father and I had several clashes, and it created a divide in our home where we couldn't meet each other without my mom's help. In the meantime, some terrible things happened that changed our lives for the better, or maybe on the right path," Pankaj said, shrugging his shoulders.

Dangerous Subconscious

"Something that breaks our hearts heals our soul."

After that moment, they started skipping exams and partying, not doing anything productive. However, one topic of discussion kept echoing in the colony.

"Dipu got a job!" Rishi announced in a circle with mixed emotions.

"Wow, how did he manage that?" Pankaj asked, curiosity evident on his face.

"His father died in service six months ago, and they offered Dipu his job. But we can't kill our own fathers for jobs," Rishi remarked, a hint of bitterness in his tone.

"What? Who would even do that?" Pankaj questioned, alarmed.

"Who knows!" Rishi said with a sly grin.

"What?" Pankaj looked at Rishi with suspicion and confusion.

"Forget it, forget it. I'll get my Ph.D. entrance results today. Let's go see whether it's good news or bad," Rishi said, changing the subject and starting his bike.

"I hope you get a good rank," Pankaj wished Rishi as he got on the bike.

"I hope so too," Rishi said with a wide smile.

They headed to Pandit Saab's shop to check the results.

At Pandit's shop, Rishi asked excitedly, "Are the results out, Pandit Saab?"

"Yeah, give me your hall ticket number," Pandit replied, looking at his monitor.

"Just tell me if it's good or bad. I don't want to lose my pride with my rank," Rishi said, silently praying.

"Okay, okay," Pandit chuckled and typed in Rishi's hall ticket number.

"Are you going to the university?" Pankaj asked, dejected, knowing he would have to leave soon too.

"Let's see what happens," Rishi said, feeling optimistic.

"Rishi, it's a big ball, a very big ball," Pandit shouted with excitement, hugging Rishi tight.

"A big ball? What do you mean?" Rishi asked, confused.

"You got the sixth rank! You're going to university! Dipu got a job! And next, it's our Pankaj!" Pandit exclaimed excitedly.

"Sixth? Are you sure that's my name?" Rishi asked Pandit, still in disbelief.

After congratulating Rishi, Pankaj felt a tinge of loneliness and whispered, "Now I will be alone, right?" Rishi reassured him that he too would find success and left to share the news with his parents. As Pankaj pondered about his own future, he couldn't help but remember Dipu and the rumors he had heard. What if his own father passed away and he was offered his job, just like Dipu? He could secure employment without having to endure his father's constant criticism and feeling unworthy. The thought lingered in his mind, tempting him with an easier path to success.

At Home

After a few days, Pankaj called Rishi to ask when he would join the university.

"Hello, State Ranker!" Pankaj greeted Rishi on the phone.

"Where have you been all these days?" Rishi asked Pankaj in a low tone.

"Preparing for exams," Pankaj replied.

"Meet me at Pandit's shop," Rishi informed and hung up.

"Okay," Pankaj said as he stared at the phone.

Later, Pankaj went to meet Rishi, but before he could, Goswami called him and said he wasn't feeling well and asked Pankaj to get him medicine. "I have things to do," Pankaj said before leaving home.

At Pandit's Shop

"Hey, Pankaj!" Rishi shouted to catch Pankaj's attention.

"Hey, State Ranker! How are you?" Pankaj greeted Rishi as he walked towards him.

"State Ranker!" Rishi sighed with red eyes.

"What happened?" Pankaj asked, looking at Rishi's face.

"Pandit ji, two beers!" Rishi signaled Pandit with his hands.

"Why are you drinking beer?" Pankaj questioned, staring blankly at Rishi's face.

"Sometimes, this is sweeter than honey. The pain that this thing causes in your throat turns out to be soothing to open your throat," Rishi stated, handing Pankaj a bottle.

"Why?" Pankaj exclaimed.

"You too hold one!" Rishi replied and placed a bottle in Pankaj's hand.

"You said you prayed for me, right? What did you pray for?" Rishi asked Pankaj.

"I asked God to give you a good rank!" Pankaj replied happily.

"Did you forget to ask for a university seat?" Rishi asked Pankaj in a low voice with a heavy heart.

"You got sixth rank amidst thousands; how come you did not get a place in the university?" Pankaj questioned, staring into Rishi's red eyes.

"This is India. Your rank, your brain, your hard work never pays off," Rishi replied, taking a sip of beer.

"You didn't get a seat?" Pankaj gasped in shock.

"How can I get one? I was not born in a lower caste or a higher caste; I was not born in a rich family or a poor family; we are in the middle, Pankaj. No one cares for us. We must hustle our lives as long as we live, and I'm tired!" Rishi uttered, staring into the sky and taking a deep breath to control his tears.

Pankaj took a sip of beer and said, "This time it's not hurting!"

"Because your heart is more bitter than this," Rishi replied with a smirk.

"I want to run away from this world, somewhere where we don't need money, caste, and job to live," Pankaj expressed his desire.

"Shall we go for a trip?" Rishi asked excitedly.

"When?" Pankaj questioned with a smirk and had another sip of beer.

"Right now!" Rishi exclaimed with sparkling eyes.

"Now? To where?" Pankaj chuckled.

"We'll plan on the way!" Rishi said and looked into Pankaj's eyes.

"Okay, let me tell my mom," Pankaj said.

"Don't tell anyone. We'll even leave our phones behind," Rishi insisted.

"Come to your senses, Rishi," Pankaj said firmly, "No, I can't. I know you want to, but my dad needs me right now."

"Okay, I'm going. Don't tell anyone," Rishi said and left.

Pankaj's phone rang multiple times, and he finally answered it. It was Lakshmi; she said that their father had a heart attack. Pankaj felt the ground give away under his feet. He was dazed momentarily, but quickly came to his senses when his mother's voice in his head wouldn't stop saying those words. He rushed to the hospital without a thought of Rishi. While standing in front of the hospital, he remembered Dipu and the bitter thought in his mind earlier. He stepped back.

The Revise

The Subconscious Realm

"Why does God replay our life from the beginning when we are on the death bed?"

Goswami had a heart attack and was taken to the hospital by his wife alone.

"Swami, look at me! Why are you staring at the ceiling? Please talk to me!" Lakshmi wailed, trying to get his attention.

"Madam, please don't shout. We will do our best. Please be seated and let us do our work. Don't worry, nothing will happen," the doctor consoled her.

Goswami was taken into the ICU, but he continued to stare at the ceiling for hours.

In His Subconscious:

Goswami stood in front of the house with his bicycle thinking about Kamal.

"Swami, I need ten lakhs," Kamal requested his brother.

"Ten lakhs? That's a huge amount! What do you need it for?" Goswami asked, shocked, inquiring about Kamal's requirements.

"There was a person called Ramesh Kalita who said he would offer me a job after paying ten lakhs," Kamal stated.

"Are you sure you will get this job?" Goswami questioned for assurance.

"Yes, brother!" Kamal said confidently.

Goswami lent ten lakhs to Kamal wishing for Kamal's bright future, but it turned out to be the biggest headache in his life.

After paying the money to Ramesh Kalita, Kalita disappeared from the town, which caused tension for Goswami. From that day until the date of his sick bed, he kept visiting and knocking on Kalita's door, only to end up disappointed because he never showed up.

At Ramesh's House

Goswami stood silently in front of the house, doing nothing. He stared at the house with hope-filled eyes. After waiting for a few hours, he relentlessly pressed the doorbell. When he got no response, he decided to knock on the door. After several minutes of struggle, a grumpy man named Raju, wearing a white vest, opened the door with a frown.

"Again?" Raju shouted with a frown.

"Did he come?" Goswami asked politely.

"Are you shameless? Or do you have amnesia? If you ring my doorbell one more time, I'll sue you mercilessly!" Raju shouted at Goswami in an impolite manner and tried to push him by holding his neck.

"I have shame, I have pride, I have children, and a loving family, but the cheater who ruined my happy life is hiding in the nooks of the world. As this is his last-known location, I was hoping to see him here one day. Please don't take my helplessness ... AAH ..." Goswami held his hand and expressed his grief.

"Shut up! I'm not interested in listening to your nonsense. Leave my house right now and never come back. This is not his resting place or your gaming zone. Get lost!" Raju pushed Goswami's hand and shut the door in his face.

Goswami returned home on his cycle with a nervous face. He lost his joy and his mind lost focus. He became inattentive to his son, his wife, and even his work. His life became secretive to the world, and he never let the world see his dark phase.

At the Market

Early in the morning, Goswami went to the market to buy some household items. He saw Pankaj's favorite fish in the market—fresh and raw.

"How much?" Goswami asked the fisherman.

"200/kg," the fisherman replied, showing his fingers.

"Isn't that too much? Can't you reduce the price?" Goswami raised his eyebrows and asked.

"Sir, you are my regular customer. Why would I use bargaining tactics on you? This is the price of the fish, and even ten rupees less would be a loss for me!" the fisherman explained as he arranged the fish.

"Is there any other fish that is fresh and within my budget?" Goswami asked the fisherman, hoping to find a smaller fish at a lower price.

"Sir, these are freshly caught fish, alive and delicious. They are from our local rivers," the fisherman said, showing him the fish.

"Local ... Salani?" Goswami asked.

"Yes, sir. Just ask madam to add light spices and let the fish cook under low flame. The taste of the fish will linger in your mouth until your next birth," the fisherman replied.

"Your words are tastier than your fish," Goswami joked with a smile.

"Have a good day, sir. Thank you," the fisherman greeted Goswami.

"Have a good day," Goswami replied and left the market.

After returning from the market, Goswami took a bath and got ready for work. He asked his wife to tie his turban, and he left for work.

At the Railway Track

Goswami and his colleague Deka went to work, carrying their hammers for track investigation. Throughout the way, they poured out their hearts to each other.

"You have been inattentive lately! Is something bothering you?" Deka questioned Goswami as they worked.

"I don't know if it's wise to share with you, but in the end, you are the only one with whom I can open up," Goswami replied with a sigh.

"Colleagues are like an unsaid family that we live together day and night," Deka replied to Goswami while checking the railway beams.

"A few months back, I borrowed ten lakhs from Baisya for Kamal's job. I gave that money to a person named Ramesh Kalita, and after we paid that money, I never saw or heard from him again." Goswami shared his grief while working on the parallel lines.

"Isn't it an unpinned grenade?" Goswami asked with a low tone.

"Kamal is your brother, right?" Deka questioned.

Goswami smiled dryly and moved forward.

"Did you get any news about the job?" Deka asked, knowing he didn't.

Goswami showed his index finger to the sky and continued working.

Deka watched him silently, knowing that one improper word might break him apart.

After working for hours in the scorching heat, Goswami returned home on his bicycle and parked it in the railway quarters. He entered his home, hung his clothes on the rope, and washed his face, feet, and hands before going inside.

"Do you want to talk about it?" Goswami asked Lakshmi with concern.

"It's nothing, just some family issues," Lakshmi replied, trying to hide her emotions.

"Don't keep it inside, share with me. We are a family, we should be there for each other," Goswami urged her.

Lakshmi hesitated for a moment but then she opened up to Goswami about the financial troubles they were facing and how she was struggling to make ends meet.

Goswami listened patiently and then hugged Lakshmi, assuring her that everything would be alright.

"Don't worry, we will get through this together. We are a family and we will always be there for each other," Goswami said with a smile.

Lakshmi smiled back, feeling grateful to have such a caring and supportive husband.

"Men hustle through life to appear tough, and forget that sharing is a way to relieve themselves from life's burdens."

Lakshmi entered the room with a glass of tea.

"Here's your red tea! Why are you staring at the ceiling? Is there a cobweb?" Lakshmi handed over the tea and looked up at the ceiling.

"Cobweb?" Goswami questioned mysteriously with a smirk on his face.

"I spend hours cleaning these webs every day, but they keep coming back." Lakshmi sighed, searching for cobwebs.

"One day this too shall pass!" Goswami murmured with a low voice.

"Some things won't pass, we must put an end to them," Lakshmi stated with a heavy breath.

"Yes, we must put an end to them," Goswami repeated with a sad face.

Goswami finished his tea and returned the empty glass to his wife.

"Turn off the lights; I'm feeling sleepy. And check on Pankaj before you sleep," Goswami instructed.

Lakshmi turned off the lights and headed to Pankaj's room. There she saw tears in Pankaj's eyes that were slowly dripping down his cheeks.

"Pankaj! Pankaj!" Lakshmi called out to Pankaj, but his ears were occupied with high-volume earphones playing acoustic music to soothe his anxiety.

Lakshmi tapped him to wake him up from his thoughts.

"What happened, Pankaj?" Lakshmi asked with a soothing voice.

"What are you doing, Maa?" Pankaj questioned his mother as he wiped his tears.

"I'm here to talk to you!" Lakshmi replied as she rubbed his head.

"Is there anything bothering you?" Lakshmi questioned, knowing that something was wrong.

"Nothing, Maa, just listening to songs." Pankaj sighed and showed his phone playing music in the background.

"When I married your father, I was scared to discuss with him the things we were dealing with together and individually. One day I missed my family so much! I went to sleep with tears in my eyes, as you did now. Then your father came in and asked what happened? I said nothing, but after a few days I remembered my grandmother's words: To reduce the weight in your heart, you must pour out your heart to your loved ones."

Lakshmi recalled her painful time with a shudder.

"I got it, Maa! But my thing is not something that can be cleared just by telling you." Pankaj pinched his eyebrows.

"It might not, but when you tell me, you'll feel you

have someone to hear your words out," Lakshmi said as she caressed Pankaj's hair, his head on her lap.

"Maa, you are also thinking that I'm useless right?" Pankaj questioned with tears in his eyes.

"I never did. And I know one day my kid is going to be the best in this town," Lakshmi conveyed her trust in her son.

"But your kid is a failure, Maa! He attended hundreds of interviews and thousands of exams but he got not even a single call letter." Pankaj wailed his grief before her mother.

"I know nothing about this, Pankaj. If things are taking time, trust the time, not your state, because time knows when you need it. The day you reach the time of receiving you can't stand on your legs." Lakshmi taught Pankaj about the game of life that stresses people.

At the Market

Goswami and Banerjee were having a lively conversation about their families and retirement when Baisya, the money lender, unexpectedly appeared on his bike. Goswami and Banerjee tried to avoid him, but he confronted Goswami about his unpaid loan.

"Goswami, why are you avoiding my calls? You remember that your loan period has long passed," Baisya warned in a high-pitched voice.

"Yes, sir, I remember. I will call you tonight," Goswami replied uncomfortably.

"I'll be waiting. Remember, respect lasts as long as you protect it. If you try to hide, the world will know that you lost your pride for money," Baisya stated loudly, drawing attention from people in the market.

Goswami gave him a blank stare and remained silent. Baisya then greeted Banerjee and left.

After Baisya left, both Goswami and Banerjee felt uneasy and parted ways with fake smiles. Goswami felt humiliated by Baisya's words and slowly made his way to the market to buy fish, before returning home on his bicycle.

After Work

He handed over his hammer to his supervisor and started working on the tracks. His mind was still occupied with the same thoughts, but he tried his best to focus on his work. After some time, his colleague Deka came to him and started talking about his day. Goswami tried to listen to him, but his mind was still wandering.

"Is everything okay with you? You seem lost today as well," Deka said, his eyes narrowed at Goswami.

"Yeah, I'm fine. Just a little distracted," Goswami replied with a sigh.

"You know, sometimes it helps to share your

problems with others. We all have our struggles, and talking about them can ease the burden," Deka advised.

Goswami nodded his head in agreement and felt a little better. As the day went on, he tried to focus on his work and forgot about his worries for a while. When he returned home, he apologized to Lakshmi for his behavior in the morning and told her about his concerns. Lakshmi listened to him patiently and assured him that they would find a solution together. Goswami felt relieved and grateful for having such a supportive partner.

At the Railway Track

"Goswami, why are you so late?" Deka questioned.

"Things are overwhelming me," Goswami murmured.

Goswami picked up his hammer and began working with Deka. They worked hard in the scorching heat until lunchtime, and during their lunch break.

"How's your blood pressure? Any improvement?" Deka asked.

"It fluctuates, sometimes high and sometimes low. And now, I think I've developed diabetes too," Goswami replied with a sigh.

"Ugh, same here! Can't we leave this world without these ailments?" Deka groaned.

"God needs a reason to call us back to him, and that's why he puts us through all these trials and tribulations in life," Goswami stated.

"Yeah, maybe you're right," Deka said.

"How's Biki? Is everything good with him in college?" Goswami asked about Deka's son.

"He's doing well, he got admission in an MBA program in Bangalore," Deka replied while taking a bite of his food.

"But sometimes, I feel like I'm losing the game of life. I'm tired of playing. I can't do this anymore. The low income, high expenses, and my kid's tuition fees are burying me in debt. Every single penny has become more precious, yet people still refuse my proposals," Deka expressed his frustration.

After hearing Deka's words, Goswami abruptly left his lunch unfinished.

"I can't eat this and even I can't throw it out when I'm not rich, and the guilt and pain are choking me," Goswami said as he got up to wash his hands.

Deka watched silently as Goswami washed his hands.

"We are the losers of the life game. But hopefully, one day our sons will break this cycle and succeed," Goswami said with hope.

After finishing work, Goswami rode his bicycle back home.

At Home

After arriving at home, Goswami changed out of his work clothes and into a dhoti. Pankaj was browsing job ads on his phone, but quickly closed it and retreated to his room. He laid on his bed playing with a Rubik's cube. He had tears in his eyes and his face was red with emotion.

"Pankaj! Pankaj!" Goswami called out, but Pankaj didn't respond and walked past him into the house.

"Come and have dinner, Pankaj," Lakshmi called out later.

Pankaj and Goswami sat together for dinner, with Lakshmi serving the food.

"How did the exam go?" Goswami asked, trying to make conversation.

Pankaj remained silent as he absentmindedly fiddled with his food.

"Why don't you try applying for private jobs? Any job that can support our family and pay off our debts is a good job," Goswami suggested, trying to help his son with his career.

"To get jobs in marketing and other fields, I need a bike. And you can't provide that for me," Pankaj finally spoke up, stating his needs for job hunting.

"Why are you treating me like your enemy? I'm trying to be a good father. Can't you take a step for your father's sake?" Goswami sighed, expressing his frustration.

As Goswami entered his room, he changed into his night clothes and laid down on his bed. Lakshmi followed him into the room with a red box that contained his pills.

"Did you take your pills?" Lakshmi asked, noticing that Goswami's shirt was wet.

"I forgot to take them," Goswami replied with a sigh.

Lakshmi handed him a glass of water and watched as he took his medication. Afterward, she sat down on the bed next to him.

"I'm worried about Pankaj," Lakshmi said softly.

"So am I," Goswami admitted. "I don't know how to help him."

"We have to be patient and understanding," Lakshmi said. "He's going through a tough time."

"I know," Goswami replied. "But sometimes it's hard to know what to say or do."

"We just have to be there for him," Lakshmi said, placing a comforting hand on Goswami's shoulder. "He needs our support now more than ever."

Goswami nodded in agreement and leaned his head on Lakshmi's shoulder. Together, they sat in silence, hoping that things would get better for their family.

Lakshmi handed Goswami his medication from the red box. "Tomorrow you must go to work, sleep without worrying. To clear the loan, let us sell the land given by my parents. It's mortgaged for up to ten lakhs."

"Do you think they will give us the whole property by trusting us?" Goswami replied with distrust.

"Let's give it a try. If it works out, great, and if not, we can sell it. I will speak with my brother," Lakshmi said confidently and with trust in her brother.

"If we fail to retrieve it, we will lose our pride in front of your family." Goswami sighed.

"Pride is not the only thing that matters in a family. I don't know about the world and other stuff, but I believe that if there is love, you need not to quit the game of life," Lakshmi said with a heart full of love.

"I'm sorry for making you both suffer with my foolish actions," Goswami showed his guilt before his family.

"Don't think too much and go to sleep," Lakshmi said to Goswami.

Goswami spent the night staring at the ceiling, considering all the possibilities of providing a bike for Pankaj. The next day, he woke up feeling dizzy and nervous but finished his morning routine and prepared for his market session. He went to the market as usual, but his words trembled while talking to the farmers and fishers.

Goswami slowly walked back to his bicycle and put everything on the handlebar. As he pedaled home, the weight on the bicycle felt heavier with each meter. The chain clanked loudly and the world around him became blurry. He eventually parked his bicycle under a nearby tree and rested his back against it. A kind young boy passing by noticed him and offered him some water.

"Uncle, are you feeling dizzy?" the boy asked.

"Kind of," Goswami replied, his words trembling and his breaths heavy.

"Here, have some water and wash your face," the boy offered, helping Goswami sit properly.

"Thank you, God bless you!" Goswami blessed the boy and drank some water from the bottle.

"Can you walk, uncle? I can drop you home if it's nearby," the boy suggested.

"Thank you, sweetheart, but I can walk," Goswami replied, still panting.

"Okay, uncle. Take some rest before you go, otherwise, you'll get weaker," the boy advised.

"Thank you very much," Goswami thanked the boy as he left.

After the boy left, Goswami slowly got up and made his way back home with a wet shirt and a strange stare. Lakshmi asked him why he came back late and what had happened to him.

"Just tired from cycling in this weather. Can you give me my washed uniform? I'm getting late for work," Goswami said as he sat on the sofa with a sweat-soaked shirt.

"Wait a moment, I will pack your lunchbox," Lakshmi said as she went into the kitchen.

"No, Lakshmi. I can't eat," Goswami replied, panting.

"You must take your pills! Have some food," Lakshmi insisted while packing his lunch bag.

"Yes, I forgot to take my medicine. Can you go get it for me?" Goswami asked.

As Lakshmi went to get his pills, Goswami's phone rang with Baisya's name on the screen. He stared at the phone, feeling anxious. His body started shivering, and his hands trembled like never before.

Lakshmi and Deka rushed Goswami to the hospital. The doctors examined Goswami and started his treatment. After a few hours, Goswami regained consciousness and was moved to a private room. Pankaj arrived at the hospital, looking worried and anxious. He went to his father's room and sat beside him.

"How are you feeling now, Dad?" Pankaj asked softly.

"I'm feeling better, son," Goswami replied weakly.

"I'm sorry, Dad, I shouldn't have spoken to you like that," Pankaj said with tears in his eyes.

"Don't worry, son. I understand how you feel," Goswami said, holding his son's hand.

"I'll take care of you, Dad. I promise," Pankaj said, with determination in his voice.

"Don't worry about me, Pankaj. You focus on your career and your future," Goswami said with a kind smile on his face.

"I will, Dad. I won't let you down," Pankaj said, with a sense of responsibility in his voice.

Lakshmi and Deka entered the room, and the family sat together, talking about their future and how they could support each other. They realized that they needed to work together to overcome their financial struggles and move forward.

The Melodrama

At the Hospital

When Lakshmi called Pankaj several times and he still didn't show up at the hospital, she asked Deka to call her brother on her behalf. Deka called Lakshmi's brother Satish and explained the situation.

"Hello, who is this?" Satish asked on the phone.

"Brother!" Lakshmi replied, crying.

"Lakshmi! Whose number is this? Why are you crying? Where is Goswami and Pankaj?" Satish asked, concerned.

"Goswami is sick and in the hospital. I called Pankaj, but he still hasn't shown up. I don't know what to do!" Lakshmi explained, still grieving.

"Okay, don't worry, I will come. But before that, hand over the phone to the person who is with you," Satish instructed.

"Sure, brother!" Lakshmi said and gave the phone to Deka, who introduced himself to Satish and explained Goswami's condition and lifestyle.

"May I know the situation there?" Satish asked.

"Sir, I don't know how to say it, but you know the state of affairs. There are no jobs, and even for those who have them, the salary is not enough to feed a person," Deka expressed the harsh reality of life.

"Yes, it's becoming increasingly difficult to sustain lives," Satish agreed.

"And for people who have loans and debts, it's like living in hell. The pressure of loan sharks, landlords, and children's educational fees is dragging them to their death beds," Deka said.

"Does Goswami have debts?" Satish questioned curiously.

"Yes, he's drowning in debt," Deka stated about Goswami.

"Lakshmi never mentioned this. Do you know how much and why?" Satish inquired deeply.

"To the best of my knowledge, it's ten lakhs," Deka said to Satish.

"Ten lakhs? Why?" Satish was shocked.

"A few years ago, Kamal asked Goswami for ten lakhs for a job, and they paid the money to someone. But the person never showed up, and their calls went unanswered," Deka explained everything to Satish.

"What about the money lender?" Satish questioned, taking a deep breath.

"He's a humble person, but he hurts people with his words to get his money back," Deka informed him about Baisya.

"Are there any other loans or debts?" Satish asked.

"All I know is this, and he's stressing out about it," Deka closed the topic.

"Okay, thank you, sir," Satish said and hung up the phone.

Satish thought of a solution and remembered his father's property, which belonged to both of them. He asked his wife Sulochana to bring the property papers and fifteen lakhs in cash. She questioned him in suspicion.

"Why do you need such a large amount suddenly?"

"I have an emergency to attend to. Please pack my bag for three days," Satish said.

"Lakshmi! How have you been?" Satish greeted his sister as he arrived.

"Satish! Long time no see. I'm doing well. How's Dheeraj and Sulochana?" Lakshmi hugged her brother in welcome.

"Where is Pankaj?" Satish inquired.

"I don't know. He's been acting strange for a few months now," Lakshmi replied.

"I need to talk to you about something," Satish said, leading her to a nearby chair.

"Sure. What is it?" Lakshmi asked.

"Do you have debts?" Satish looked at Lakshmi.

"We made one wrong decision, and now we're stuck in a pit," Lakshmi confessed, chewing her lip.

"Just one phone call, and your brother could've helped you out of this pit," Satish assured her.

"I know, but …" Lakshmi hesitated.

"Wait, I'm not helping you this time," Satish interrupted.

Lakshmi looked at her brother with a blank expression.

"You remember that dad left us a villa," Satish reminded her about their property.

"Yes," Lakshmi nodded.

"If I give you the papers, you can mortgage the land for fifteen lakhs. But you might not be able to repay it, and we could lose the land. Right?" Satish explained with a sly grin.

Satish then proposed two options. "I can either give you fifteen lakhs without the need to repay by signing over the property documents or you can take the property documents and repay the fifteen lakhs."

Lakshmi was confused and didn't know what to do. "We must save Goswami right now, but he needs to clear that ten lakhs debt to get better," Satish explained. "You can either get a mortgage on the property or take the fifteen lakhs from me and the property will be mine forever. It's up to you to make a wise decision."

"I don't know whom to ask for a mortgage," Lakshmi said innocently.

"So, you will take the fifteen lakhs and leave the property?" Satish asked, happy to have her agree to his plan.

Lakshmi understood the game, but she remained silent. Her only wish was for her husband and son's peace of mind. She signed the property documents and thanked her brother.

After the documentation, Satish left saying that Dheeraj was sick.

The Restoration

Together

Pankaj waited patiently for Baisya to finish his calculations. After a few minutes, Baisya handed over the papers to Pankaj and said, "Here are the documents, and the total amount with interest is twelve lakhs. You have to pay this amount within six months, or else the interest will increase."

Pankaj's face fell as he heard the amount. "Uncle, how can it be twelve lakhs? We borrowed only ten lakhs," he said in disbelief.

Baisya replied, "Yes, but you didn't pay the interest on time, so it has accumulated over the months. It's all there in the documents."

Pankaj realized his mistake and apologized to Baisya. He promised to repay the entire amount with interest within six months. Baisya gave him a stern look and said, "I hope you keep your promise, or else you will face the consequences."

Pankaj left Baisya's home feeling ashamed of his actions. He knew he had to work hard to repay the debt and make things right for his family.

At the Hospital

Pankaj and Lakshmi entered Goswami's room where he was lying down. Goswami looked weak, his face was pale and his eyes were closed.

"How are you feeling now?" Lakshmi asked with concern.

"I'm feeling better, but weak," replied Goswami in a feeble voice.

"Did you eat anything?" asked Pankaj.

"No, not yet," replied Goswami.

"I'll go and get something for you to eat," said Pankaj as he left the room.

"Do you need anything else, dear?" asked Lakshmi, holding Goswami's hand.

"No, I just need to rest," replied Goswami, closing his eyes.

Lakshmi sat beside Goswami and watched him as he slept. She couldn't help but feel anxious about their financial situation and how they would pay for everything. She prayed for a miracle to happen, but deep down she knew that they had a long road ahead of them.

As Pankaj looked at his weak and pale father, his eyes filled with tears and love. He walked straight to his father and hugged him.

"Don't you hate me?" Goswami asked with tears in his eyes.

"I never hated you, Papa. I'm just frustrated because I can't help you." Pankaj wept, hugging his father tightly.

"Good things won't come easily. What comes easily goes easily," said Goswami, rubbing Pankaj's head.

"You said you don't trust me. From then, I lost my courage. Do you really not trust me?" Pankaj asked Goswami nervously.

"I trust you more than I trust myself. That day, I was scared that you may end up like Dipu, drinking and scolding his dead father. I was scared you might hate me even after my death," Goswami replied.

"No, Papa, never," Pankaj said, wiping his tears.

Lakshmi looked at them happily and packed everything. Meanwhile, Deka arrived to check on them.

"How are you doing, Goswami?" Deka greeted as he nervously entered the room.

"I'm fine, brother. How's work treating you?" Goswami replied.

"It's the same old, same old," Deka responded with a dull expression.

"Ah, I see," Goswami sighed.

"Can I get my money back?" Deka asked abruptly.

"Money?" Goswami questioned, confused.

"Yes, I paid for the tests and medicine that the doctors prescribed," explained Deka.

"How much was it?" Goswami inquired.

"For the tests and all, it was 20,900 rupees, and for food, travel, and ambulance, it was another 5,000 rupees. But since you are like a brother to me, 5,000 rupees is enough," Deka replied, handing over the bills he had.

Lakshmi immediately gave Deka twenty thousand rupees, saying it was all they had.

"Where did you get this money from?" Goswami asked blankly.

"We'll talk about it later. Just give the money to him and tell him that we will pay the rest from our bonus money," Lakshmi whispered in Goswami's ear.

Goswami relayed the message to Deka, who reluctantly accepted. Later, they left the hospital and headed home.

At Home

Lakshmi intervened, "Yesterday, Satish came here and helped us clear the loan. He gave us the option to mortgage our property or take the money and give him the property. We chose the latter, and now the property belongs to him, but we have the money to pay off your hospital bills and other debts."

Goswami looked at Lakshmi in disbelief and said, "I didn't know about this. You should have consulted with me before making such a big decision."

"I did what I thought was best for our family. We needed the money, and Satish was willing to help," Lakshmi explained.

Goswami sat there in silence for a moment and then said, "I'm grateful for Satish's help, but we need to find a way to get our property back."

"We'll figure it out, but for now, let's focus on your health and getting back on your feet," Lakshmi said.

Pankaj nodded in agreement, and they all continued with their dinner.

"Today itself! My brother came to make a deal without asking, and I was surprised; then I got it. All he wants is that property, not his sister; he tried to pour honey on the wound and stabbed us from the back," Lakshmi expressed her pain.

"Did he insult you?" Goswami asked with concern and a heavy heart.

"Thankfully, he didn't insult me. He took the whole house using this situation," Lakshmi said, dejected, wiping her face with her saree.

"Then why didn't you question him?" Pankaj asked in anger.

"At that moment, your father and you felt more important to me than that property," Lakshmi stated.

"No one is worth trusting," Pankaj raged.

"That is life," Goswami said to Pankaj. "And this is just the beginning," Lakshmi added.

They finished their dinner and headed back to their rooms to sleep.

Early in the morning, Pankaj woke up anxiously and went into his father's room. He stared at his sick father and went back to his room.

"Maa! Do you want me to bring anything? I'm going to the market," Pankaj said to his mother.

"Bring some vegetables. Come here; I will give you money," said Lakshmi.

"Okay, wait," said Pankaj and walked to his room. He changed into a t-shirt and shorts with slip-ons, then went back to Lakshmi to receive the money.

"Maa, give it. I will go and get the vegetables," Pankaj said and walked into the kitchen along with his mother.

Lakshmi took out five ten-rupee notes from a spice bottle and handed them to Pankaj.

"Fifty rupees?" Pankaj exclaimed in shock.

"Yeah," Lakshmi confirmed.

Pankaj realized how he used to spend money on unnecessary things and realized that his father was no different—struggling in his own way.

The Insult

At the Market After a Few Months

Goswami went to the market and stopped at a tea shop to have some tea. He sat on a backless cement bench and blew on the hot tea to cool it down. As the steam from the tea dissipated, someone's face across from him became clearer. Goswami was shocked for a moment before quickly finishing his tea and running after the person. As soon as the person realized Goswami was chasing him, he started running as well. After a few minutes, Goswami caught up to Kalita.

"I won't let you go even if I die!" Goswami said to Kalita.

"Please, let go of my collar. People are watching!" Kalita begged.

"I won't let you go even if I get arrested," Goswami replied, still holding onto Kalita's collar.

"Okay, do you want me or my shirt?" Kalita asked, trying to trick Goswami.

Goswami let go of Kalita's shirt, and they both stood panting and bent over for a few minutes.

"Where is my money?" Goswami asked Kalita aggressively.

"I won't build villas with your money! It's all going toward administration," Kalita replied recklessly.

"I don't want any job. I just want my money back. If you don't return my money within a week, I won't go easy on you," Goswami warned Kalita with a fierce gaze.

"Everything is in process, even your brother's job. Don't rush things," Kalita tried to deceive Goswami.

"I don't want any job. Please, I just need my money back urgently," Goswami stressed to Kalita in the market.

As the crowd began to take notice of their conversation, Kalita became aware of his reputation and said, "Fine, take that money with your bonus on that day. I'll return it to you before everyone else."

They parted ways, and on his way home, Goswami's phone rang loudly. With the morning sun behind him, he struggled to look at the screen before answering.

"Hello?" Goswami answered.

"Goswami! It's Deka," came the reply.

"Hello, Deka *bhai*. How are you?" Goswami asked excitedly.

"I'm good, but it's been months, and you still haven't returned my money," Deka said, frustrated.

"Deka *bhai*, things aren't going great for me right now. I'll return your money for sure, but please understand my situation," Goswami tried to explain.

"No one is having a good day, neither you nor me. But you have to repay the money that you took, right?" Deka shouted at Goswami, not listening to his excuses.

"I understand, *bhai*. I will return your money as soon as I receive my bonus," Goswami replied in a low voice.

"I won't listen to you! If you don't return my money, I will come to your house!" Deka shouted aggressively before hanging up.

Goswami sighed, knowing that he couldn't convince Deka over the phone. He slowly pedaled his bicycle back home.

At Home

Lakshmi prepared rice for lunch and breakfast for both Pankaj and Goswami, while Pankaj sat by the window in his room, observing everything. Goswami returned from the market, struggling to untangle the bag from the handlebars of his bicycle. Just then, the postman arrived at the gate, overtaking Goswami with an envelope in his hand. Pankaj rushed to the main door, excited to see what it was.

"What is it?" Pankaj asked the postman eagerly.

The postman struggled to read the envelope, but Pankaj grabbed it and read the name on it aloud.

"Arindom Bagchi!" Pankaj exclaimed, his face turning red. He returned the envelope to the postman with a serious expression and went back to his room.

Meanwhile, Lakshmi entered the hall.

"Pankaj, what's wrong with your behavior?" Lakshmi shouted at him.

"It's okay, ma'am," the postman said to Lakshmi.

"May I know who you are looking for?" Lakshmi questioned the postman.

"It's Arindom Bagchi, there is a call letter in his name," the postman said.

"It's the next door," Lakshmi said, pointing to the next door with her hand.

"Thank you," the postman greeted.

Lakshmi folded her hands straight to her heart to convey her welcome for his thanks. As she walked to the kitchen, she glared at Pankaj who was aggressively playing with a Rubik's cube.

After a while, Pankaj gave up on the Rubik's cube and left home.

Meanwhile, Goswami left for work, taking his bank book, debit card, lunch box, and water bottle in separate polythene bags.

At the ATM

Goswami stopped at the ATM with Baisya and Kalita. Kalita was speaking with some tea laborers while counting money. The labor man was taking some time to complete his transaction, and Goswami politely asked him to hurry up so that others could use the ATM too. But Kalita tried to stop the labor man from moving and manipulated him to take his time, saying that it was a public ATM and Goswami had no right to order him around.

When Baisya mentioned that Pankaj had cleared his loan, Kalita mocked him, trying to bring Baisya in. But Goswami explained that he was thinking of the people standing outside in the heat, and that he would never insult anyone.

As Goswami waited for his turn, Kalita ignored him and kept counting money, staring at Goswami in an evil manner. When Baisya asked why Goswami needed a loan again after clearing it months ago, Kalita and Baisya tried to abuse him, making fun of his financial situation and his health.

Goswami tried to explain that he was not borrowing any money, but Kalita continued to provoke him. Finally, Kalita offered to give Goswami the money he had allegedly asked for, all the while speaking sweetly in front of everyone. Goswami felt humiliated and insulted in public, and slowly pedaled his bicycle away from the ATM.

As he was returning home, he saw Pankaj crying in the tea garden. He rushed to him and asked him what was wrong. Pankaj wiped his tears and said it was nothing, but Goswami persisted and asked him again. Pankaj finally opened up and said that he felt like a bad dream was chasing him while his life dreams were sleeping.

Dreams Come True

"Kalita returned the money!" Goswami said to Pankaj.

"What!" Pankaj exclaimed with a happy face.

"Yeah! Here is the money. Let's go home and give this money to Mom, then we will meet Deka and repay his money, and finally go to the showroom and get a good bike. Okay?" Goswami cheered Pankaj.

Pankaj hugged his father tightly, and cried loudly. Then they left for home together. Goswami gave the entire amount to Lakshmi and then took some back for the bike and to repay Deka.

Pankaj and Goswami were preparing to leave for Deka's house. At that moment, Pankaj received a call.

"Hello!" Pankaj answered nervously.

"Hello, am I speaking to Pankaj?" the recruiter asked.

"Yes, sir!" Pankaj replied anxiously.

"We are calling from TCS, the company where you interviewed for the Associate Software role in Guwahati, Dispur. We are very pleased to inform you that you were selected for it."

"Thank you, sir!" Pankaj replied with a small blush.

"Can we discuss your salary?" the recruiter asked.

Pankaj continued the call, his face getting redder with every passing second. After the call ended, he said, "Papa, I got the job!"

"Lakshmi! Lakshmi!" Goswami shouted loudly.

Lakshmi rushed out anxiously, running towards them.

"Maa! I got a job in a big company; it's really big." Pankaj rejoiced with his parents.

Lakshmi hugged her son with tears and blessed him.

While they were celebrating his moment, Deka entered the scene and got frustrated seeing Goswami happy.

"Do you have any shame on your face, Goswami?" Deka shouted loudly.

Goswami looked at Deka with surprise at his harsh words.

"I understand that you helped us during tough times, but that doesn't give you the right to speak to us in that manner. We were just on our way to meet you when I received a call from the interviewer, which delayed our arrival." Pankaj spoke up, feeling hurt by the way his father was being treated.

"Anyway, you are here now, and we have good news to share. Pankaj got a job and we are returning your money. Let's not waste this moment by worrying and instead celebrate together," Goswami said, trying to diffuse the tension. He handed over the money to Deka.

Deka's expression softened, and he nodded in agreement. They joined together to celebrate Pankaj's achievement, forgetting the bitter words exchanged moments ago.

The Parallel

Present Time at the Railway station

"I have some doubts," Srinu said.

"Am I giving a lecture or what?" Pankaj joked.

"No, the thing is there is a dream that's been haunting you. And what happened to your friend Rishi? Where did you go in those two days when your father was sick in the hospital?" Srinu asked, persistent.

"You're listening to my story like you're going to write it down." Pankaj laughed.

"I'm not, but you have to clear my doubts," Srinu said.

"The dream that haunted me! I told you, the subconscious is dangerous. When Rishi used the phrase 'We can't kill our fathers to get a job,' I started having a dream that four people were carrying my father on their shoulders, and I just felt anxious every time. I used to wake up suddenly with a heavy head and a painful heart. After I got my job, those dreams vanished over time," Pankaj explained.

"So, you didn't go to the hospital because of this dream?" Srinu asked.

"Kind of. If something happened that day, I might not have forgiven myself till now," Pankaj replied with a wry smile.

"And what about Rishi? Where did he go?" Srinu asked.

"He just took a small trip that turned into a long journey. He ended up in a foreign country and now works as a teacher there," Pankaj replied.

"It's really heartbreaking that even with a sixth rank, he couldn't get a seat in any university," Srinu said, expressing his dissatisfaction.

"That's how our country works; your intelligence means nothing before your caste in India," Pankaj said, vocalizing his dismayed opinion about their country.

"And where did you go in those two days while your father was in the hospital?" Srinu asked, raising another question.

"I went to the tea garden, tried to console myself, wept like a small kid for my father, and slept over there. I had that dream again, and when I woke up, I ran to the hospital, and you know the rest," Pankaj explained.

"Okay, let's go now. We forgot about the time while talking," Srinu said, and they headed to the railway station. They got on Srinu's bike and rode to Pankaj's home.

"Pankaj! Why are you so late?" Lakshmi questioned.

"I'm not a kid, Maa! You are still treating me like one," Pankaj replied, blushing at her love.

"Even though you have become a father, you are still my son. Go wash your hands and legs," Lakshmi said, taking his bag and arranging water for him to wash.

Lakshmi called his wife Leela to assist him.

"Why did you come home so late? You were supposed to bring the kids from school! Get ready, and bring them home," Leela whispered as she walked to him.

"Srinu and I ended up talking about things from the past. It's been five years, but they still whirl in my mind as if they just happened," Pankaj replied.

"Reminding oneself of the past is both good and bad. Don't dwell too much in the past, and cherish your present," Leela advised Pankaj.

"Okay, dear. Can you bring me my bike keys?" Pankaj asked Leela.

Leela went into the room to get the keys.

"Here are your keys. Go fast and bring the kids home," Leela said.

Pankaj drove his sons back home from school and Leela changed their clothes and gave them some snacks. Then, they sat down to study and Pankaj helped them with their reading.

Abhi, Pankaj's first son, asked, "Papa, tell me about the 'father of the nation.'" Pankaj was reminded of his own childhood when he had asked the same question to his father. He looked at his father with joyful eyes, and Goswami looked back at Pankaj and smiled.

Pankaj and Goswami are parallel to each other. They have suffered together, grown together, and lived together. Although they have traveled on different paths with different worries, they have remained parallel in their lives. Hence, they are called Parallels.

All characters in this book are fictitious and bear no resemblance to anyone or any person in original.

This is an in-house publication of Ukiyoto Publishing.

www.ukiyoto.com

www.ingramcontent.com/pod-product-compliance
Lightning Source LLC
LaVergne TN
LVHW041633070526
838199LV00052B/3335

9789360161590